The Rooster Crows

A Book of American Rhymes and Jingles

Maud and Miska Petersham

Aladdin Books
Macmillan Publishing Company New York
Collier Macmillan Publishers London

Aladdin Books
Macmillan Publishing Company
866 Third Avenue, New York, NY 10022
Collier Macmillan Canada, Inc.

First Aladdin Books edition 1987

Printed in the United States of America

A hardcover edition of *The Rooster Crows* is available from
Macmillan Publishing Company

10 9 8 7 6 5 4 3

Library of Congress Cataloging-in-Publication Data
Petersham, Maud Fuller, 1890–1971.
The rooster crows.
Summary: A collection of traditional American nursery
rhymes, finger games, skipping rhymes, jingles, and
counting-out rhymes.
1. Nursery rhymes. Children's poetry, American.
[1. Nursery rhymes. 2. American poetry] I. Petersham,
Miska, 1888–1960. II. Title.
PS586.3.P47 1987 398'.8 87-1138
ISBN 0-689-71153-0 (pbk.)

Contents

Bye, baby bunting.
Father's gone a-hunting;
Mother's gone to milk a cow;
Sister's gone–I don't know how;
Brother's gone to get a skin
To wrap the baby bunting in.

I asked my mother for fifty cents
To see the elephant jump the fence.
He jumped so high
He reached the sky
And never came back till the Fourth of July.

How much wood would a woodchuck chuck
If a woodchuck could chuck wood?
A woodchuck would chuck as much as he would chuck
If a woodchuck could chuck wood.

Had a mule, his name was Jack,
I rode his tail to save his back.
His tail got loose and I fell back,
Whoa, Jack!

Mary had a little lamb,
Its fleece was black as tar.
And everywhere that Mary went
They thought it was a b-a-a-r.

Engine, engine, Number Nine,
Running on Chicago Line.
If she's polished, how she'll shine,
Engine, engine, Number Nine.

Trot, trot to Boston
To buy a loaf of bread.
Trot, trot, home again,
The old trot's dead.

Johnny on the woodpile,
Johnny on the fence,
Johnny get your hair cut
Fifteen cents.

There was a little man,
He had a little gun,
He put it in his pocket,
And away he did run.

This little pig goes to market,
This little pig stays home,
This little pig has roast beef,
This little pig has none,
This little pig cries "Wee, wee, wee!"
All the way home.

Lady bug, lady bug,
Fly away home.
Your house is on fire,
Your children are gone.
All but one and her name is Anne,
And she crept under the pudding pan.

Star bright, star light,
First star I've seen tonight.
Wish I may, wish I might,
Have the wish I wish tonight.

A bear went over the mountain,
A bear went over the mountain,
A bear went over the mountain
To see what he could see!

The other side of the mountain,
The other side of the mountain,
The other side of the mountain
Was all that he could see.

Wake up, Jacob,
Day's a-breakin',
Peas in the pot
An' hoecake a-bakin'.

One I love,
Two I love,
Three I love I say,
Four I love with all my heart,
Five I cast away.
Six he loves,
Seven she loves,
Eight they both love.
Nine he comes,
Ten he tarries,
Eleven he courts,
Twelve he marries.
Thirteen they quarrel,
Fourteen they part,

Fifteen he dies of a broken heart.

Two's a couple,
Three's a crowd,
Four on the sidewalk
Is never allowed.

One, two, three,
The bumble bee,
The rooster crows
And away he goes.

Red at night,
Sailors delight.
Red in the morning,
Sailors take warning.

A knife and a fork!
A bottle and a cork!
That's the way to
Spell New York!

A chick in a car!
And a car won't go!
That's the way to
Spell Chicago!

M, I, crooked letter,
Crooked letter, I,
Crooked letter, crooked letter,
I, P, P, I,
And this spells Mississippi.

I eat my peas with honey,
I've done it all my life.
It makes the peas taste funny,
But it keeps them on my knife.

Peter, Peter, pumpkin eater,
Had a wife and couldn't keep her.
He put her in a pumpkin shell
And there he kept her very well.

Jack and Jill went up the hill
To fetch a pail of water.
Jack fell down and broke his crown,
And Jill came tumbling after.

Patty-cake, patty-cake, Baker's man,
Bake me a cake as fast as you can.
Roll it up and roll it up
And put it in the pan.

Little Miss Muffet sat on a tuffet,
Eating her curds and whey.
Along came a spider and sat down beside her
And frightened Miss Muffet away.

Tickle'e, tickle'e on the knee,
If you laugh, you don't love me.

Shoe the old horse,
Shoe the old mare,
But let little coltie
Go bare, bare, bare.

Bat, bat, come under my hat,
And I'll give you a slice of bacon.
And when I bake, I'll give you some cake,
That is, if I'm not mistaken.

Mackerel sky, mackerel sky,
Never long wet, never long dry.

Rain before seven,
Clear before eleven.

Evening red and morning gray
Sends the traveler on his way.
Evening gray and morning red
Brings down rain upon his head.

A B C D goldfish?
L M N O goldfish.
O S A R goldfish.

Little Jack Horner sat in a corner,
Eating his Christmas pie.
He stuck in his thumb and pulled out a plum
And said, "What a good boy am I!"

Way down yonder on the Piankatank,
The bull frog jumped from bank to bank
And skinned his leg from shank to shank,
Way down yonder on the Piankatank.

I came to the river and I couldn't get across,
Paid five dollars for an old blind hoss.
Wouldn't go ahead, nor he wouldn't stand still,
So he went up and down like an old sawmill.

I'm going to Lady Washington's
To get a cup of tea
And five loaves of gingerbread,
So don't you follow me.

Hushabye,
Don't you cry,
Go to sleepy, little baby.
When you wake
I'll give you cake
And lots of pretty horses.
One will be red,
One will be blue,
One will be the color of Mammy's shoe.
Hushabye,
Don't you cry,
Go to sleepy, little baby.

I see the moon,
And the moon sees me.
God bless the moon,
And God bless me.

Black cat sat on the sewing machine
Looking fine and handsome,
Ran ninety-nine stitches in his tail
And then he ran some.

I had a dog,
His name was Rover.
Every time I looked at him
He turned over and over.

There was a little girl
And she had a little curl
That hung right down on her forehead,
And when she was good
She was very good indeed,
But when she was bad she was horrid.

Yankee Doodle went to town
Riding on a pony,
Stuck a feather in his hat
And called it Macaroni.

First's the worst,
Second's the same,
Last's the best of all the game.

A flock of white sheep
On a red hill,
Now they stamp, now they champ,
Now they stand still.

Where was little Moses when the light went out?
Under the bed with his feet sticking out.

I climbed up the apple tree
And all the apples fell on me.
Make a pudding, make a pie,
Did you ever tell a lie?
Yes, you did. You know you did,
You broke your mother's teapot lid.

The ark is made of gopher wood
And in it there are gophers two,
But if you go for a gopher,
A gopher will go for you.

Adam and Eve and Pinch-me-tight
Went out in the river to bathe.
Adam and Eve were drowned-ed.
Who do you think was saved?
Pinch-me-tight.

Fuzzy Wuzzy was a bear,
Fuzzy Wuzzy lost his hair.
Then Fuzzy Wuzzy wasn't fuzzy,
Was he?

One, two, three, four, five,
Once I caught a fish alive.
Six, seven, eight, nine, ten,
Then I let him go again.

Why did I let him go?
Because he bit my finger so.
Which finger did he bite?
The little one upon the right.

I have a little sister, they call her "Peep, Peep,"
She wades in the ocean deep, deep, deep,
She climbs up the mountain high, high, high,
The poor little thing has only one eye.

Rich man,
Poor man,
Beggar man
Thief.
Doctor,
Lawyer,
Merchant,
Chief.

As sure as the vine
Twines 'round the stump,
You're my darling sugar lump.

Monday's child is fair of face,
Tuesday's child is full of grace,
Wednesday's child is full of woe,
Thursday's child has far to go,
Friday's child is loving and giving,
Saturday's child works hard for a living,
But the child that is born on the Sabbath day
Is blythe and bonny and good and gay.

Mother, may I go out to swim?
Yes, my darling daughter.
Hang your clothes on the hickory limb,
But don't go near the water.

The rose is red, the violet's blue,
Sugar's sweet and so are you.
If you love me as I love you,
No knife can cut our love in two.
My love for you will never fail
As long as pussy has a tail.

Finger Games

Here is the bee-hive,
Where are the bees?
Hiding away where nobody sees.
They are coming out now,
They are all alive.
One! Two! Three! Four! Five!

These are Mother's knives and forks
And this is Mother's table.
This is Mother's looking glass
And this is baby's cradle.

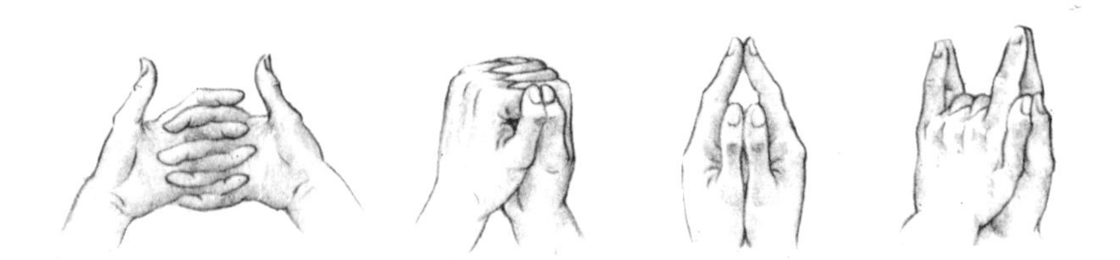

Five little rabbits went out to walk;
They liked to boast as well as talk.
The first one said, "I hear a gun!"
The second one said, "I will not run!"
Two little ones said, "Let's sit in the shade!"
The big one said, "I'm not afraid!"
Bang, bang! went the gun,
And the five little rabbits ran, every one.

There were two blackbirds
Sitting on a hill,
The one named "Jack"
And the other named "Jill."
Fly away, Jack,
Fly away, Jill,
Come again, Jack,
Come again, Jill.

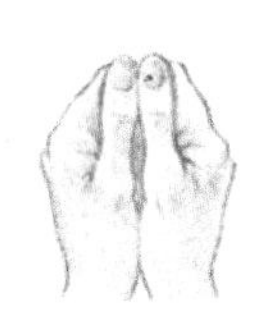

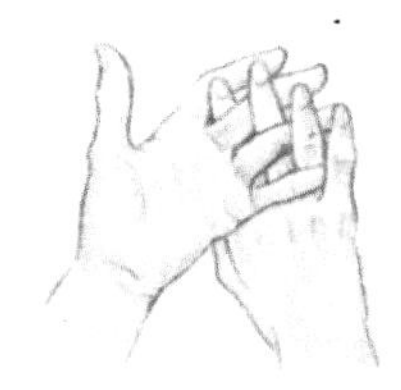
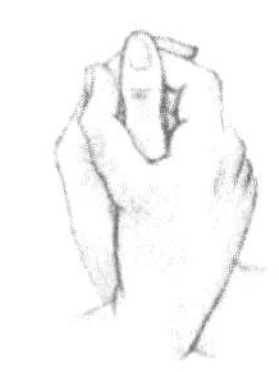

Here is the church, here is the steeple,
Open the door and see the people.
Here are the singers going upstairs,
And here is the minister saying his prayers.

Rope Skipping Rhymes

Granny, Granny I am ill,
Send for a doctor to give me a pill.
Doctor, Doctor, shall I die?
Yes, you must and so must I.
How many carriages shall I have?
Ten, twenty, thirty (count until skipper misses).

1, 2, 3, 4, 5, 6, 7,
All good children go to heaven.

Miss, miss, Little Miss, miss,
When she misses, she misses like this.

Teddy Bear, Teddy Bear, turn around,
Teddy Bear, Teddy Bear, touch the ground.
Teddy Bear, Teddy Bear, show your shoe,
Teddy Bear, Teddy Bear, that will do.

Teddy Bear, Teddy Bear, go upstairs,
Teddy Bear, Teddy Bear, say your prayers.
Teddy Bear, Teddy Bear, switch off the light,
Teddy Bear, Teddy Bear, say Good Night.

Counting-out Rhymes

Entry, kentry, cutry, corn,
Apple seed and apple thorn.
Wire, brier, limber lock,
Three geese in a flock.
One flew east, one flew west,
One flew over the cuckoo's nest.
O-U-T spells out goes she.

Hacker, packer, soda cracker,
Hacker, packer too.
Hacker, packer, soda cracker,
Out goes you.

Onery, uery, ickory Ann,
Filisy, folasy, Nicholas John,
Queever, quaver, English neighbor,
Stinkem, stankem, B-bo-buck.

One potato, two potatoes,
Three potatoes, four,
Five potatoes, six potatoes,
Seven potatoes more.

Bushel of wheat,
Bushel of rye.
All not ready, holler "I."

One, two, three,
Look out for me,
For I am coming
And I can see.

Games

Oats, peas, beans and barley grows,
Oats, peas, beans and barley grows,
How, you nor I nor nobody knows,
Oats, peas, beans and barley grows.

Thus the farmer sows his seed,
Stands erect and takes his ease,
Stamps his foot and clasps his hands,
And turns about to view his lands.

Waiting for a partner,
Waiting for a partner.
Open the ring and take her in
And kiss her when you get her in.

Now you are married you must obey,
You must be true to all you say,
You must be kind, you must be good,
And keep your wife in kindling wood.

Ring around a' rosies,
Pocket full of posies.
Sweet bread, rye bread,
Squat!

Quaker, Quaker, how is thee?
Very well, I thank thee.
How's thy neighbor next to thee?
I don't know, but I'll go see.

All around the buttercup,

One, two, three!

If you want a pretty friend,

Just choose me.

Lazy Mary, will you get up,
Will you get up, will you get up?
Lazy Mary, will you get up,
Will you get up today?

What will you give me for breakfast
If I get up, if I get up?
What will you give me for breakfast
If I get up today?

A slice of bread and a cup of tea.

No, Mother, I won't get up,
I won't get up, I won't get up.
No, Mother, I won't get up,
I won't get up today.

A nice young man with rosy cheeks.

Yes, Mother, I will get up,
I will get up, I will get up.
Yes, Mother, I will get up,
I will get up today.

Bean porridge hot,
Bean porridge cold,
Bean porridge in the pot
Nine days old.

Some like it hot,
Some like it cold,
Some like it in the pot
Nine days old.

I-tisket, I-tasket,
A green and yellow basket,
I wrote a letter to my love,
And on the way
I dropped it, dropped it, dropped it.
A little boy came and put it in his pocket,
In his pocket, pocket, pocket.

Little Sally Waters,
Sitting in the sun,
Crying and weeping
For a young man.

Rise, Sally, rise,
Dry your weeping eyes,
Fly to the East, fly to the West,
Fly to the one that you love best.

Yankee Doodle

Fath'r and I went down to camp
Along with Captain Good'n,
And there we saw the men and boys
As thick as hasty puddin'.

And there was Captain Washington
Upon a slapping stallion,
A-giving orders to his men
I guess there was a million.

I saw a little barrel, too,
The head was made of leather.
They knocked upon 't with little sticks
And called the folks together.

And there I saw a swamping gun,
Big as a log of maple,
Upon a mighty little cart,
A load for father's cattle.

And every time they shoot it off
It takes a horn of powder
And makes a noise like father's gun
Only a nation louder.

It scared me so I hooked it off,
Nor stopped as I remember,
Nor turned about till I got home
Locked up in mother's chamber.

Chorus
Yankee Doodle, keep it up,
Yankee Doodle dandy,
Mind the music and the step
And with the girls be handy.